Clue Jr.

The Case of the Secret Password

Look for these Clue™ Jr. books!

The Case of the Secret Password

Book created by Parker C. Hinter

Written by Della Rowland

Illustrated by Diamond Studio

Based on characters from the Parker Brothers game

A Creative Media Applications Production

SCHOLASTIC INC.

New York Toronto London Auckland Sydney

ISBN 0-590-13785-9

Copyright © 1997 by Hasbro, Inc. All rights reserved. Published by Scholastic Inc. by arrangement with Parker Brothers, a division of Hasbro, Inc. CLUE ® is a registered trademark of Hasbro, Inc. for its detective game equipment.

12 11 10 9 8 7   2/0

Printed in the U.S.A.   40

First Scholastic printing, August 1997

Contents

The Case of the Secret Password

Introduction

Meet the members of the new Clue Club. Samantha Scarlet, Peter Plum, Greta Green, and Mortimer Mustard.

These young detectives are all in the same fourth grade class. The thing they have most in common, though, is their love of mysteries. They formed the Clue Club to talk about mystery books they have read, mystery TV shows and movies they like to watch, and, also, to play their favorite game, Clue Jr.

These mystery fans are pretty sharp when it comes to solving real-life mysteries, too. They all use their wits and deductive skills to crack the cases in this book.

You can match *your* wits with this gang of junior detectives to solve the eight mysteries. Can you guess who did it? Check the solution that appears upside down after each story to see if you were right!

The Case of the Blue Handprint

Every Saturday morning, Mortimer Mustard, Greta Green, Peter Plum, and Samantha Scarlet meet for their Clue Club meeting. Each week the meeting is at a different member's house. During the meeting, the Clue Club kids discuss their favorite mystery movies and books, and decide how to spend their club dues. At the end of each meeting, they play Clue Jr.

This Saturday the weekly meeting was at Greta's house. As the kids were finishing their lunch, Mrs. Green announced that she would drive them to the movies that afternoon.

"I know there's a new mystery movie you all want to see," she told them. "And it's my treat." The kids cheered.

"The movie starts in half an hour, so we should get going soon," Mrs. Green added.

"Before we go, I need to check on my rabbits, Mom," said Greta.

"Okay," Mrs. Green said. "But don't be long."

The kids put their plates and glasses in the sink and followed Greta out the back door.

Greta's father had built her two rabbit cages in the backyard that summer. A soft brown rabbit was napping in one cage. In the other, a pure white rabbit was munching on some lettuce.

"Hi, Ginger," Samantha said to the brown rabbit. The rabbit woke up when Samantha poked a carrot through the wire.

"When did you get two rabbits, Greta?" asked Peter.

"This one's not mine," said Greta, petting the white rabbit with her finger. "I'm just keeping it in the extra cage for Betsy Blue while her family is on vacation. I'm getting another one, though — as soon as Betsy takes Ralph home."

Just then, several little kids came through the gate. "There's Tommy, Rachel, Sarah, and Jackson. They live on my street," Greta whispered to the other Clue kids. "They always want to play with the rabbits."

"We're having a party," Jackson told Greta.

"Do you want to come?" asked Rachel.

"Thanks, guys. Maybe later, okay?" said Greta. "We're going to the movies now."

"Can we play with the rabbits, Greta?" asked Tommy.

"You can later, when I get home from the movies," Greta said.

The children reluctantly walked back through the gate. "I let them hold the rabbits sometimes," Greta told her friends. "The only problem is, they want to play with them all the time!"

Samantha looked at her watch. "Uh-oh.

We'd better hurry or we'll miss the beginning of the movie," she said.

"We need time to get our popcorn, too," said Mortimer.

"Okay," said Greta. "Mom's probably already in the car."

"Race you," said Peter as they all took off for the car.

On the way back from the movie, Greta asked the other Clue kids if they wanted to go back to her house to help her feed the rabbits. "Yeah!" everyone said at the same time.

When they got to her house, Greta gave everyone some lettuce and carrots to carry outside. As soon as they got near the cages, they noticed something was strange.

"Someone switched the rabbits, Greta," Samantha said.

"The rabbits are in the wrong cages!" Peter said.

"You're right," said Greta. "What happened here?"

"It seems like someone took the rabbits out," said Mortimer.

"And look," shouted Peter, "whoever it was left handprints!"

Greta leaned down to look at the cage. There was a smudge of bright blue paint on the pen door.

"Hey, there's a blue handprint on the white rabbit, too," said Samantha.

"Oh, no," cried Greta. "I better get it off before Ralph starts cleaning himself. The paint could hurt him." She ran into the house and came back with soap, a pan of water, and a sponge.

"Blue paint," said Peter. "Are any of your neighbors painting their houses?"

"No," said Greta.

"Maybe it was one of your parents," said Samantha. "Let's go see."

The kids ran into the house to see if Mr. or Mrs. Green had painted anything blue that day.

Mr. Green was in the den watching a football game on TV. He looked up from the

7

set. "Nope," he said. "I haven't painted anything in months. If I'm lucky I'll never have to paint anything ever again," he chuckled. "Ask your mom, sweetheart. She's in the greenhouse."

The kids ran out to the greenhouse where Mrs. Green was potting plants. She hadn't done any painting either. Plus she hadn't been near the rabbits all day.

"Looks like you have a mystery on your hands," Mrs. Green said.

"Sort of," said Mortimer. He held up his hand. "We have a mystery handprint."

The Clue kids went back to the rabbit cages to see if they could find any more clues. After a while, they saw the neighborhood kids peering over the fence. "Is it okay to play with the rabbits now?" Rachel called out.

"I guess so," Greta said. "Come on over and I'll take them out."

"Can we show you the pictures we made at our party, Greta?" asked Jackson.

"Sure," Greta answered. "We can hang them on the fence."

Greta took Ginger out of the pen and carried her over to Jackson and his friends. The Clue kids followed with some vegetables.

"Can we hold the white rabbit, too?" asked Sarah.

"Well, the white rabbit doesn't belong to me," said Greta. "Someone took her out today while I was gone."

"And I think I know who it was," said Samantha.

"Who?" said Greta.

"It was you, Tommy," Samantha said. "Right?"

How does Samantha know Tommy took the rabbit out?

Solution
The Case of the Blue Handprint

Tommy nodded. "How did you find out?" he asked.

Samantha pointed to his finger painting. "From your finger painting," she said.

"I get it," said Peter. "Jackson and his friends came over here after they made their finger paintings. Tommy opened up the pen and took out the rabbits."

"But he didn't wash off his finger paint first," said Mortimer. "So Tommy left handprints on the cage door."

"And on Ralph," said Greta.

"And you put the rabbits back in the wrong cages," said Samantha.

"Oh," said Tommy. "Are you mad, Greta?"

"Only a little," said Greta. "I just don't want anything bad to happen to the rabbits. So from now on, just wait for me to open the pens. Okay?"

"Okay," promised Tommy. The other three kids nodded too.

"Looks like we solved the case of the hand-painted rabbit," laughed Greta.

The Case of the Creepy Crawlies

Mortimer's cousins, Sidney and Shirley, were visiting for a week during summer vacation. Since the cousins had never been camping, the Mustards decided to take them on a camping trip. They invited the Clue Club kids to come along, too.

"Are you guys ready to rough it?" Mrs. Mustard asked them as they drove to the campsite.

"I guess," said Shirley. "I've never slept outside in a tent before."

"It'll be fun," said Mr. Mustard. "My favorite part is cooking our meals over a fire."

"Yeah. Food tastes really great when it's cooked over a fire," Mortimer told them.

"And every day we'll hike to a different

spot," said Mrs. Mustard. "This park is full of trails and beautiful waterfalls."

"And there's a lake we can go swimming in," Mortimer said.

Mrs. Mustard turned into the state park and drove to their campsite. After unpacking the car, they set up three tents — one for Mr. and Mrs. Mustard, one for Mortimer, Peter, and Sidney, and one for Greta, Samantha, and Shirley.

By the time the tents were up, everyone was tired, and Mortimer was starving. The Mustards put all the food in large sealed containers.

"You're very organized," Shirley said to Mr. Mustard.

"You have to be when you're camping out," he replied. "But we don't do this just to be organized," said Mr. Mustard. "There's a better reason for putting our food in sealed containers. It keeps rodents and insects from getting at the food."

"Yeah, the first time we went camping, it was a mess," laughed Mortimer. "We wound up living with raccoons and squirrels and all kinds of bugs."

When everything was unpacked, the Mustards cooked some stew over the fire. After dinner, Mr. Mustard told ghost stories until everyone fell asleep.

The next morning, the group was up early.

"Look," cried Samantha. "Tracks." She pointed to some animal tracks around the campsite and on top of the containers.

"Looks like some raccoons and squirrels were here," said Mrs. Mustard.

"Good thing you brought these sealed food containers," said Samantha. "They really work."

That day, the kids hiked through the woods to a waterfall where they had lunch. Later, Mortimer helped Mr. Mustard make hamburgers over the fire.

"You're right, Mortimer," said Greta. "Everything tastes better when it's cooked over a fire."

*　　*　　*

That night, everyone wanted to go to sleep early because they were tired from hiking. "Tomorrow we'll hike to the lake, where we can swim," Mrs. Mustard told the kids as she put out the fire and said good night.

The next morning, Mr. Mustard found one of the containers open and ants were crawling in and out of it.

"Oh, no! Now how did this happen?" exclaimed Mr. Mustard.

"Do you think an animal opened the container?" asked Peter.

"Probably," answered Mr. Mustard.

"There were tracks everywhere yesterday," said Greta. "But I don't see any this morning."

"Doesn't look like much is missing though," said Mrs. Mustard, peering into the container. "Nope, just a package of cookies."

"Why didn't the animals take everything in the container?" asked Samantha.

"They should have," said Mrs. Mustard,

frowning. "The ants have gotten into everything else in the container. We'll have to throw it all away."

"Well, we'll just make a trip into town sometime today to get some more supplies," said Mr. Mustard.

"Can we still go swimming in the lake?" asked Mortimer.

"Probably not," said Mr. Mustard. "It'll take a while to get to town, shop, and drive back. And we have to clean up our campsite to get rid of the ants."

"Why don't we see a movie in town so the day isn't a waste?" suggested Mrs. Mustard.

The kids cheered and got busy cleaning up.

Later that afternoon, when they returned from town, Mr. Mustard gathered the kids together. "Check your tents to make sure everything is okay," he told them. "We don't want any creepy crawlies taking over our camp."

"All quiet on the home front," Peter said,

after the kids had gone through their tents.

"You mean the camp front," laughed Greta.

"My sleeping bag's okay," said Mortimer.

"Mine, too," Shirley piped up.

"No invaders here, sir," said Samantha, giving Mr. Mustard a salute.

"Good work, troops," Mr. Mustard laughed.

"Since it's too late to go to the lake, let's hike up to the ridge," suggested Mrs. Mustard. "It overlooks the lake and we can watch the sunset from there."

The sunset looked like orange sherbet splashed across the blue sky. Samantha took some photographs. When they got back to the camp, everyone was tired. So they fixed a quick dinner and got ready for bed.

"I'm going to make *sure* the food containers are closed before we go to sleep," said Mr. Mustard. He checked them carefully, then stood up. "Looks good. Good night, everyone," he said and started for his tent.

Suddenly a scream came from the boys' tent. Everyone ran to the tent to see what was going on. Sidney was standing over his sleeping bag, pointing down.

"What's wrong?" cried Mortimer as Mr. and Mrs. Mustard peered into Sidney's sleeping bag.

"I don't know yet," said Mr. Mustard. "Hand me a flashlight." When he pointed the flashlight at the sleeping bag, Peter started laughing.

"What's so funny about Sidney screaming?" exclaimed Greta.

"Well, now we know who opened the food container last night," laughed Peter. "It was Sidney."

How does Peter know Sidney opened the food container?

Solution
The Case of the Creepy Crawlies

"How did you know, Peter?" asked Shirley.

Greta laughed and pointed to the sleeping bag. "The ants told him," she giggled.

"Sidney must have dropped cookie crumbs in his sleeping bag," smiled Samantha. "Looks like the ants found them."

"Is that true?" Mr. Mustard asked Sidney, trying not to smile.

"Yes," said Sidney, looking down at the ground. "I guess I didn't shut the lid on the container tight enough. I'm sorry."

"I think you should be responsible for cleaning up the camp after dinner tonight," Mr. Mustard said sternly. "The first thing you can do is shake out those ants." Then he began laughing. "But not in the tent!"

At that everyone burst out laughing — even Sidney. Mortimer and Peter helped him fold up his sleeping bag. Then they carried it away from the campsite to shake out the ants.

"That's what happens when you try to 'squirrel' something away on a camping trip," laughed Mortimer.

The Case of the Cool Clues

Mortimer tossed his beach bag into the back of the Plums' minivan. Then he climbed into the backseat beside Peter. "Your parents are really cool," he told Peter.

"Especially when it's hot," giggled Samantha. She and Greta were sitting in the middle seat of the van.

It was the middle of August. The temperature had been one hundred degrees for more than a week. So Mr. and Mrs. Plum had decided to take Peter and the rest of the Clue Club to the beach to cool off for the day.

Mr. Plum shut the back door of the van and climbed into the driver's seat. "We're off!" he announced. "Next stop, THE

BEACH!" Everyone cheered as the van rolled out of the driveway.

Forty-five minutes later, they could hear the waves hitting the beach. Before he parked the van, Mr. Plum drove past the boardwalk. There were souvenir shops selling seashells and T-shirts, a card shop, shuffleboard stand, pizza and ice cream parlors, restaurants, and even a movie theater.

"Wow, this place has everything!" cried Peter.

On the beach, kids were surfing on their boogie boards, playing volleyball, and building sand castles.

After swimming and searching for seashells, the kids headed off for the boardwalk. They played some video games, ate pizza, and wound up at the ice cream parlor.

"Let's have some ice cream," Mortimer suggested. "Then we'll be cool inside and out!"

The kids ordered ice cream cones and sat

down at a table near the window. Just as they were finishing, a kid sitting at the table next to theirs got up and quickly walked out.

"Did you see that?" whispered Samantha, shocked. "He didn't pay for his ice cream."

"I saw," said Greta.

"And so did the owner," said Peter. The apron-clad shop owner ran past them and out the door after the kid.

The Clue kids paid for their ice cream and headed back to the beach.

"There's our spot," said Samantha. She pointed to the place where they had left their beach towels.

"Isn't that the kid who didn't pay for his ice cream?" asked Mortimer. He was looking at a boy standing on the beach along with two adults and another boy.

"Yeah," said Greta. "And he's with the guy who owns the ice cream parlor."

"Looks like they're talking to a beach guard," said Peter. As they got closer, they could hear the boy and the shop owner arguing.

"This kid ran out without paying for his ice cream," the owner was telling the beach guard.

"How could I?" said the boy. "I wasn't even in your shop this afternoon. I've been playing volleyball with my friend for the last half hour."

"That's right," the other boy told the beach guard. "He's on my team."

"I don't know what I can do," the beach guard said to the shop owner. "It's your word against his. And he has someone else saying he wasn't in your store. Maybe it *was* someone else."

"Wait," said the owner, pointing to the Clue Club kids. "Those kids were in the shop at the same time. Come over here, please!"

The owner asked them if they'd seen the boy in the store.

"Yes, we did," said Greta.

"We saw him walk out without paying, too," said Samantha.

"It must have been somebody who looked like me," said the kid. "Nobody can prove I was there."

"Maybe not," said Mortimer. "But I can prove something else."

"Oh, yeah," said the kid. "What's that?"

"I can prove that you probably haven't been playing volleyball for the last half hour," said Mortimer.

How does Mortimer know the kid wasn't playing volleyball on the beach?

Solution
The Case of the Cool Clues

"If you were in the ice cream parlor, how do you know that I wasn't on the beach?" the kid asked Mortimer.

"Because you're too cool," said Mortimer.

"Oh, yeah," said Peter. "Cool inside and out."

"That's right," agreed Greta. "It's one hundred degrees. If you were playing volleyball for a half hour you'd be dripping with sweat. But you're not."

"Right," said Samantha. "Just look at your friend. Even his shirt is soaked."

"You're cool from being in my air-conditioned store eating my cold ice cream," complained the shop owner.

"They've got you there, Mr. Cool," said the beach guard. "What's your story now?"

"The end of the story is one dollar and seventy-five cents," said the shop owner.

"That's what he owes me for his ice cream soda."

"If I were you, I'd pay up and avoid any further trouble," said the guard.

"Yeah, then this story will have a happy ending," laughed Peter.

The Case of the Green Clues

The town was having a fund-raiser to collect money for a kids' playground in Flannel Park. Anyone could set up a booth in the park. Since the event was being held on Labor Day, the theme of the fund-raiser was "work."

A week before the fund-raiser, the Clue Club kids were in the pizza parlor discussing the event and deciding what they could do to help. Greta decided to set up her lemonade stand. Peter wanted to put up a basketball hoop and charge a nickel a shot.

"Mortimer, we can run a Clue Club booth," said Samantha. "Whatever we make, we can donate to the park."

"Aren't you a bunch of little goody-

goody kiddies," came a voice from the next table. It was Richie Royal, the town bully.

"Aren't you going to help raise money for the park?" asked Samantha.

"Why should I?" Richie answered. "The park ain't for me, it's for little kids. I'll never use it. Why should I help to pay for it?"

"Can't you ever just help anyone else?" said Peter.

"Yeah, and I'm going to help myself to more pizza," Richie said. He got up, ordered a slice, and walked out eating it.

The next day the Clue Club kids and their parents went to a meeting for the fund-raiser. They found out the town council had given the fund-raiser a new theme.

"Since money and the park are both green, we're making green the theme of the fund-raiser," the mayor announced. "Everyone should give their booths or displays a green theme." He held up a sign with the new slogan. It read HELP MAKE OUR PARK A GREEN PLAYGROUND!

After the meeting, the Clue Club kids were at Mortimer's eating ice cream and discussing the new green theme.

"I know what I'll do!" exclaimed Greta. "I'll paint my lemonade stand green. Instead of lemonade, I'll serve limeade because it's green."

"Yeah," said Samantha. "And use ice made with green food coloring."

"My dad will help me make some green cupcakes with green icing," said Mortimer. "We can sell those at our Clue Club booth, Samantha."

"I've changed my mind about the basketball hoop," announced Peter. "I think I'll put up a golf course instead. Get it? Green? A golf course is called a green?"

"We know, Peter," said Mortimer. "That's a great idea."

"I'll ask my dad if I can use his practice 'green.' It's a piece of plywood with holes in it and it's covered with green felt," Peter explained.

"You can call the game Green Golf," Samantha laughed.

"That's a perfect name," said Peter. "I can't wait till next week. Mortimer's right. This is going to be fun."

On the day of the fund-raiser, everyone turned out, and the Clue Club kids were very busy with their booths. At five o'clock, the fund-raiser ended. Everyone began to take down their booths. Greta's parents took the limeade stand apart. Mr. Plum took the putting green away while Peter collected all the golf balls. Just as they were loading the last golf clubs into the Plums' minivan, Officer Lawford came walking through the field with Richie Royal.

"Some folks say they saw Richie shooting off firecrackers downtown — near the hospital," Officer Lawford told the kids' parents. "But Richie claims he's been here."

"I was," Richie insisted. "I'll tell you what I did." He began describing all the things he did at the fund-raiser that afternoon.

"I threw some darts at the balloons. And I dunked the clown a few times." Richie scratched his head. "Let's see, I shot some of the Clue nerd's basketballs. What else? Oh, yeah. Then I had some doughnuts and some of her lemonade," he finished, pointing to Greta.

"Nobody here remembers whether they saw him," said Officer Lawford. "It's been too busy."

"I don't remember seeing Richie either," said Mortimer. "But I'm positive he wasn't here."

"What?" yelled Richie. "If you're so positive, prove it!"

How does Mortimer know Richie wasn't at the fund-raiser?

Solution
The Case of the Green Clues

"Yes, Mortimer, how do you know Richie wasn't here?" said Officer Lawford.

"Because he doesn't have a green clue about any of the booths here," said Mortimer.

"I get it," giggled Samantha. "Richie didn't know the theme had changed to GREEN."

"Right," said Peter. "If you had really come to the fund-raiser, Richie, you'd know that my booth was a golf booth not a basketball booth."

"And you'd know that I was serving limeade, not lemonade, at my stand," said Greta.

Caught in a lie, Richie admitted to setting off firecrackers. "But it's a holiday!" he whined. "That's what firecrackers are for!"

"You know there's an ordinance against setting off firecrackers in town," Officer

Lawford said sternly. "Especially near a hospital! Get ready to pay a fine plus do some community service work, Richie!"

"Hey, Richie's finally going to do some work!" said Peter.

"And it won't be any fun!" laughed Samantha.

The Case of the Poster Project

Mortimer, Samantha, Peter, and Greta stood at the edge of the schoolyard waiting for Lee Lavender and Brian Blush. The Clue Club kids had teamed up with Lee and Brian to work on a project for their health class. They had decided to make a poster of a food pyramid, and Lee had invited them to her house to draw the poster.

"I hope they hurry," said Mortimer, looking at his watch. "School has been out ten minutes. I'm starving. I want to stop at the candy store on the way to Lee's and get a Snick-Snack Bar."

"Here comes Brian," said Samantha, pointing to the school's front door.

"Hey, guys," said Brian, running up. "Where's Lee?"

"There she is," said Peter. He nodded toward the corner of the school where Lee was talking to another student. She waved and ran over.

"Ready?" she said. "Let's head to my house."

Mrs. Lavender greeted them at the front door. She was wearing a flannel shirt and a pair of overalls that had green grass stains on the knees.

"So you're going to make a chart of the food pyramid," she said. "Why don't you all sit at the dining room table where you'll have more room to draw." Everyone sat down and began to take their health books and poster paper out of their book bags.

"If you need anything, I'll be in the back-yard," Mrs. Lavender said. "I'm pulling up all the ivy that's growing under the apple trees. What a job!" She sighed and went into the kitchen.

As the kids discussed their project, Peter took a pencil box out of his book bag. "I brought a bunch of new colored pencils and pens to draw with," he said proudly.

"My parents just bought them for me. Plus, this new pencil box. See, it's shaped like Foxy Mulligan."

When Peter held up his pencil box, everyone oohed and aahed. Foxy Mulligan was Peter's favorite basketball player — and everyone else's, too.

"Wow," whispered Brian. "It looks just like Foxy!"

"Foxy is my favorite," said Lee. "And not just my favorite basketball player. He's my favorite player period!"

"Yeah, mine too," said Brian. "He's awesome!"

"Me three," said Greta. "When he goes for a basket, he flies!"

"Don't you already have a pencil box shaped like a baseball bat?" asked Samantha.

"I did," said Peter. "But I lost it."

"Oh, Peter, you would lose your feet if they weren't attached to your shoes," laughed Greta. Everyone else laughed, too. Peter was famous for putting his things somewhere then forgetting where he left them.

"We're here to make a food pyramid," Mortimer reminded everyone.

"Oh, yeah," giggled Samantha. "Leave it to Mortimer to remember anything that has to do with food."

Lee brought a yardstick from the kitchen closet and they got to work. After they had finished the chart, Lee offered to microwave some popcorn.

"Ummm! Popcorn!" sighed Mortimer. "That sounds great." All the kids got up to stretch.

"Why don't you all go sit in the living room while I make the popcorn?" she suggested. Everyone went into the living room where they noticed a kung fu movie by the VCR.

"Lee, may I borrow your Woo Sun video?" asked Greta. "I haven't seen this one."

"Sure," Lee called from the kitchen. "Does anyone want juice?"

Everyone did, of course. "I'll help you

carry the glasses," said Samantha, going into the kitchen. After pouring juice into the glasses, Samantha carefully carried the drinks to the other room. "I'm going to look for another snack," Lee said. She opened several drawers and cabinets, looking for something else to eat.

"Great" she exclaimed. "We've got some chocolate chip cookies, too."

"Did you say you were baking cookies?" Mortimer called from the living room. "No," Lee said. "I'm not allowed to use the oven without my parents. Besides, my mom is cooking something in the oven. I'm checking on it now."

When the popcorn was finished, Lee poured it into a bowl. Leaving the kitchen, she almost bumped into Samantha, who was going back through the kitchen door for more juice. "Whoa!" Lee screamed. Mortimer jumped up and grabbed the bowl of popcorn before Lee spilled it.

"That was close," he said, scooping out a handful.

"Samantha, will you grab the salt?" Lee called. "There's a shaker near the stove."

"Sure," said Samantha. She reached for the salt shaker. "Do you want the cookies, too?" she asked.

"Oh, yeah," said Lee. "Bring them."

Samantha stuck the bag of cookies under her arm. Then she grabbed the salt shaker with one hand and a glass of juice with the other and went back to the living room.

"Mmmmm. Nothing tastes as good as popcorn," sighed Brian.

"Especially with butter," smiled Mortimer, licking his fingers.

As the kids were eating, Lee's mom came in from the backyard. "Ripping out all that old ivy is a bigger job than I thought," she told them as she poured herself a glass of juice. "Oh, your poster looks great!"

"Why don't we leave it here and I'll take it to school tomorrow," said Lee. "Mom, can you give me a ride?"

"Sure, honey," her mother answered.

"Well, I guess I should get home," said Samantha.

"Me too," said Peter. "Thanks for letting us come, Mrs. Lavender."

As the kids headed out the door, Mortimer checked his watch. "How about a quick stop at the pizza parlor?" he said. "Dinner isn't for another couple of hours."

"After all that popcorn?" laughed Samantha. "Mortimer, your stomach is amazing!"

Just then, Peter discovered his pencil box was gone. "I must have left it inside," he said.

"You also left your hat," said Samantha, pointing to his head.

Peter grabbed his head. "Oh, yeah. I left it on the couch."

The kids turned and Peter knocked on Lee's door. When she answered the door, Peter asked her if she had seen his pencil box.

"No, but come on in and look around,"

she said. "Maybe you left it somewhere and I didn't see it."

Peter got his hat, but the pencil box was nowhere to be found. "I hate to say this but maybe Brian took it," said Lee. "Foxy is his favorite player, too."

"Wow, you're right," said Peter. "I guess we should go ask him."

Just then Mrs. Lavender came in from the backyard. "You know, Lee," she said, "it's going to take me a while longer to pull out all the ivy. I'd like to finish it today, so maybe we'll just get some takeout food tonight for supper. Okay?"

"Yes!" cried Lee. "Chinese food!"

"Good idea," her mom agreed. "I'll call in an order soon."

"What about your dinner in the oven?" asked Samantha.

"Oh, it's too late to cook anything now," Mrs. Lavender said, walking out the back door.

Lee turned to Samantha. "Ssshh," Lee

hissed. "Don't remind my mom about the food in the oven or we won't have Chinese."

"I don't think there is any food in the oven," said Samantha.

"What do you mean?" asked Lee.

"Maybe there's something in there," said Samantha. "But it's not dinner."

"What is it then?" asked Lee.

"Maybe it's Peter's pencil box," said Samantha.

Why does Samantha think Lee hid the pencil box in the oven?

Solution
The Case of the Poster Project

"Why do you say that?" asked Lee.

"For one thing, your mother isn't cooking anything in the oven," said Peter.

"And your oven isn't even on," said Samantha, pointing to the temperature gauge. "See? It's off."

"Since the oven is off, I'm sure it's okay to open the door and see what's in there," said Mortimer. He pulled the oven door down and peeked in. Then he reached inside and grabbed something. Turning around, he held up Peter's pencil box.

"Samantha was right," said Mortimer.

"Foxy is my absolute favorite player," Lee said, looking down at the ground.

"Then get your own Foxy pencil box," said Mortimer. "It was pretty low to take Peter's."

Peter put his pencil box into his book

bag. "At least I didn't lose it this time," he said. "Thanks, Samantha."

"Yeah, you cooked up a good solution to this oven mystery, Samantha," laughed Greta.

The Case of the Secret Password

Mortimer hung up the phone and immediately dialed Samantha. "We've got a case," he told her.

"Cool!" exclaimed Samantha. "What is it?"

"I'll explain when we get there," Mortimer said mysteriously.

"Get where?" asked Samantha.

"Craig Copper's house," Mortimer answered. "Call Greta and I'll call Peter. Meet me at Craig's in half an hour."

Within thirty minutes, the four Clue Club kids were at Craig Copper's house ready to solve a case.

Craig was waiting for them on his front porch. "Hey, everyone," he said. Mortimer and Greta grabbed porch chairs while

Peter and Samantha sat down on the porch steps.

"So what's the problem, Craig?" asked Peter.

"It's my brother Cal," said Craig.

"Oh," said Greta, nodding her head. "Now what?" Craig and Cal were twins. But they looked different and acted very different, and often they didn't get along.

"Well, Cal and I have to share a lot, like the same room," began Craig. "Our parents really believe in this sharing thing." He sighed. "The problem is, Cal doesn't believe in sharing." The Clue Club kids nodded their heads.

"So what's the mystery you want us to solve?" asked Samantha.

"Well, last week my parents bought us a computer," Craig said, breaking into a big grin. "Wait till you see it! It's great."

"Sounds neat, Craig," said Peter. "But what's the computer got to do with Cal?"

"Oh," Craig said. "Well, the problem is, I

never get to use the computer. Cal's always hogging it."

"That's a drag," said Greta.

"I know!" said Craig. "He thinks he can use it more because he's a computer whiz."

"That's not fair," said Mortimer. "Won't he show you how to use it?"

"No way!" said Craig, waving his hands in front of him. "And this morning he set up a password on the computer and he didn't tell me what it is. Now I can't get into any of the programs."

"Have you tried typing in his name?" asked Samantha. "A lot of people use their name for the password. Or they spell their name backwards."

"Tried it," said Craig. "I tried every word I could think of that Cal might come up with. None of them worked."

"What do your mom and dad say?" asked Peter. "Can't they make him tell you what the password is?"

"Mom's at work and won't be home till

later," said Craig. "Dad's working in the backyard, but I don't want to tell him."

"Why not?" asked Greta.

"It doesn't do any good," said Craig. "They get angry at Cal, then he does something else to me. It will be better if I just figure out the password myself."

"I guess we should go see what we can do," said Mortimer, shrugging his shoulders.

Craig held the front door open while the kids filed into the house. "Our room is upstairs," he said, pointing to the staircase. "Follow me."

The computer in Cal and Craig's room sat on a small table between two desks. On the other side of the room were two twin beds. The computer was turned on and a message on the screen was asking for the password.

"Hot dog. Hot dog," said a shrill voice. Everyone turned to the corner of the room where the voice was coming from. A large

wire cage hung from the ceiling. Inside were two parakeets. One was green and gold, and the other was pale blue and white.

"Oh, cool," exclaimed Samantha. "I love birds. I have two at home. I didn't know you had some!"

"Yeah," said Craig, smiling. "Mine is the green one. His name is Sherman. I got him this spring. Sherman is about the only thing Cal and I don't share. The blue one belongs to him, but she doesn't talk much."

"I'm Sherman," the parakeet called out. "Hello. Hello. I'm Sherman. Wheet! Wheet!"

Everyone laughed.

"Hee! Hee!" tweeted Sherman. "I'm Sherman. What's for lunch? Lunchtime. Wheet! Wheet!"

"Wow!" shrieked Peter.

"Wow," whistled Sherman. "Wheet! Wheet! I'm Sherman."

"Hey, he repeated what I said!" exclaimed Peter. "What a cool bird."

"A cool bird," repeated Sherman. "I'm Sherman."

"Did you teach him to do that?" asked Samantha.

"Some of it," said Craig, laughing. "Sometimes he just repeats what he hears other people saying."

Just then Cal came into the room. "Hey, move out of the way. I need to use the computer," he said, rubbing Craig's head.

Craig frowned, brushing Cal's hand away. "I'll figure the password out," he said. "And when I do, I'll install my own password so you can't use it."

"Sure you will," snorted Cal. "Like you know how. You can't even figure out this one. Come on. I even left a clue for you on your screen saver."

"I'm Sherman," chirped Sherman.

"Shut up, Sherman," Cal snapped. "Your bird never shuts up, Craig. Doesn't he get on your nerves?"

"Shut up, Sherman," repeated Sherman.

"You're just jealous because you can't

get your bird to talk," said Craig. "You ought to spend some time teaching it."

"I'd rather spend my time on the new computer," Cal said, smirking.

"Come on, Cal, what's the password?" asked Craig.

"No way," said Cal. "Maybe your little mystery friends can solve this one for you."

"Actually, I bet I do know what the password is," said Greta.

"Okay, what is it?" asked Cal.

"I'll type it in," said Greta. She bent over and typed in a word. Immediately, the computer opened up.

"You did it!" cried Craig. "How did you figure it out?"

How did Greta discover the password? What is it?

Solution
The Case of the Secret Password

"A little bird told me," laughed Greta. "Plus Cal."

"What?" asked Craig.

"I get it," said Samantha. "Sherman."

"Right," said Greta. "But Cal also gave us a clue." She pointed to the ketchup bottles on the screen saver.

"Then Sherman told her the password!" exclaimed Peter. "It's something that goes with ketchup."

"Oh! Hot dog," said Craig.

"Hot dogs. Mmmm," said Mortimer, licking his lips.

"Right!" said Greta. "Cal said the password out loud when he was putting it into the computer. Sherman heard him and started repeating the word."

"And *I* repeat. Your bird talks too much," said Cal, storming out of the room.

"Sherman saved the day," said Craig, rubbing his bird's beak with his finger.

"Sherman saved the day," chirped Sherman happily.

"You can say that again, Sherman," laughed Samantha.

7

The Case of the Empty Birdhouse

The Saturday Clue Club meeting was held at Samantha's house. After the meeting, the Clue Club kids discussed what they were doing for their spring science projects due next week. The projects were supposed to be about something that had taken place over a period of time.

"I'm going to bake bread in a toaster oven to show how yeast makes the dough rise," said Mortimer.

"I'm doing a project on how the shape of a football changed from round to pointed on each end," Peter told the kids.

"Really? I didn't know footballs used to be round," said Mortimer.

"Mine is going to show how cotton goes from a plant to a T-shirt," said Greta proudly.

"I'm doing mine on two pairs of birds I've been watching in the backyard," said Samantha.

Samantha loved birds. In addition to her pet parrot and parakeet, she also had two birdhouses in her backyard. Each year, she put bird food out to attract wild birds so she could watch them. At the beginning of spring, a pair of robins and a pair of bluebirds had made nests in her birdhouses.

"There are some bluebirds in the birdhouse next to the garage," Samantha told the kids. "And there's a pair of robins in the other birdhouse. I think both females are sitting on their eggs."

"How can you tell?" asked Mortimer.

"First the birds carried twigs and leaves through the hole in each birdhouse to make a nest," explained Samantha. "Now the females rarely come out, and the males fly back and forth with food."

"How do you know what's going on?" Peter asked. "Do you look in the birdhouses to see the nests?"

"Oh, no!" Samantha exclaimed. "If you do, the birds will leave."

"What do you mean?" asked Greta. "Isn't that their home?"

"Yes, but if they know someone has been messing around with it, they'll find another home," said Samantha.

"This is a perfect science project for you," said Greta. "You're the bird girl!"

"I know." Samantha smiled. "I began keeping a journal of the birds after I first noticed them. The birds are from the same family, but the robins are much bigger. So of course their nest is bigger."

"I didn't know robins and bluebirds were in the same family," said Mortimer.

"Yeah," Samantha went on. "They both have red breasts, too. But the robin is brown and the bluebird is blue."

"Blue. That's what color robin eggs are too, right?" said Greta.

"Well, they're actually greenish-blue," said Samantha. "Bluebird eggs are the pale blue ones."

Samantha pulled out a book and flipped to a page featuring birds' eggs. "Here's what robin eggs look like," she said. The kids peered at the greenish-blue eggs on the page. Then Samantha pointed to a photo of bluebird eggs.

"My dad is going to make color copies of these pictures for me," Samantha continued. "I'm going to mount them on a board for my science project."

"I bet you get an A," said Peter.

"Wow!" said Mortimer, turning the page in the book. "Look how big these ostrich eggs are!"

The kids thumbed through the book, then Samantha read some of her journal to them.

A few days before the report was due, Samantha's bluebirds suddenly disappeared. Every day after school she looked out her window for hours, but there was no sign of them. One day at lunch she told the others that the bluebirds had disappeared.

"What happened to them?" Peter asked. Samantha shrugged. "I don't know."

"Have you looked inside the birdhouse?" asked Mortimer.

"No, I didn't want to bother the nest in case they come back," said Samantha. "But I will if they don't come back before my project is due."

The day before the science project was due, the bluebirds still hadn't returned. That evening Samantha finally peeked into the birdhouse. The nest was gone. That night she wrote the last entry in her journal: "The end of my project is a mystery. The bluebird nest disappeared and the bluebirds flew away."

The next morning when the students brought in their projects, Ms. Redding had them line them up on a long table. "Now I want everyone to walk by the table and take a good look at all the projects," she told her fourth grade class. "Tomorrow we'll begin our oral reports, and I'd like everyone to be familiar with the projects."

"Samantha and Jasper Jade have a lot in common," Mortimer said to the Clue Club kids as they walked by the table. "His science project is on birds' nests, too."

"Hey, you've got a couple of birdhouses in your backyard, Samantha," said Jasper. "How come you didn't bring in a nest?"

"Because they had birds in them," said Samantha. "Where did you find your nest, Jasper?"

"In my grandmother's yard," Jasper replied. "I watched the robins build the nest. Then they left for some reason, so I took the nest for my project. Lucky for me it still had the eggs in it."

"Someone probably bothered their nest and that's why they flew off," said Samantha. "That happened to the bluebirds in my backyard."

"Bluebirds?" said Jasper. "But I thought robins laid blue eggs."

"They don't, Jasper," said Greta. "And I know why you're worried about that fact."

"What are you talking about?" said Jasper.

"I'm talking about you taking Samantha's bluebird nest," said Greta.

How does Greta know Jasper took Samantha's bluebird nest?

Solution
The Case of the Empty Birdhouse

Ms. Redding walked over when she heard the children arguing. "Greta says I stole a bird nest from Samantha," Jasper complained. "But she can't prove that!"

"Well, I can prove that your nest doesn't belong to a robin," said Greta.

"How so?" asked Ms. Redding.

"Look at Samantha's photos," Greta said.

"She's right," said Mortimer. He pointed to two of the photos. "There's a robin's nest and there's a bluebird's nest. Look at the difference."

"Right," said Peter. "The robin's nest is bigger than the bluebird's."

"And the eggs are a different color," said Samantha.

"Now look at the nest Jasper brought in," said Greta.

"They're right. This is a bluebird nest, Jasper," said Ms. Redding.

"That means you didn't watch the birds at all," said Samantha. "If you had, you would have known the difference. For one thing, bluebird eggs are blue and robin eggs are greenish-blue. That's pretty easy to see."

"Where did you get this nest, Jasper?" asked Ms. Redding. "Did it really come from your grandmother's backyard?"

"No. Greta's right," said Jasper. "I didn't have a project ready so I took a nest from one of Samantha's birdhouses. I thought it was a robin's nest because the eggs were blue."

"Shame on you for taking a bird's nest while the birds were using it," said Ms. Redding. "I'm going to give you a science grade that will make you blue, too."

8

The Case of the Missing Charm

Miss Harmony's music school was having its annual music recital. Miss Harmony's students ranged from first- to eighth-graders, and all the Clue Club kids were taking lessons there. Today was their first recital, and they were all a little nervous. Samantha was playing a violin solo. Peter had a trumpet solo. And Mortimer and Greta were playing a piano duet.

Everyone at the recital was dressed up. Samantha was wearing a new dress, and Greta's mother had fixed Greta's hair in a French braid. Peter and Mortimer were both wearing suits and ties.

Miss Harmony told everyone to meet in the warm-up room next door to the recital hall. There they could tune their instruments and go over their pieces. Everyone was told to put their instrument cases on a large table in the center of the warm-up room. Instead, Samantha carried her case over to a window seat in a far corner of the room. She opened the case and took out her violin.

"Why are you all the way over there?" Peter asked. "Miss Harmony said we should put our instruments on this table."

"I can get to my violin easier this way," Samantha replied.

Greta sat down at the piano and plunked a key, and Samantha began to tune her violin. When she finished, she put her instrument back in the case and walked back to the piano.

"Look at your footprints," laughed Peter. He pointed to Samantha's shoe prints in the thick plush carpet.

"Wow," said Samantha, looking behind her. "It looks like they just vacuumed the carpet."

Just then Gloria Garish came into the room and walked over to the large table.

She shoved another student's violin case to one side. Then she put her violin case down in its place.

"See?" Samantha whispered to her three friends. "That's why I put my violin over there."

Gloria opened her case and put her violin under her chin. "Could I have an A?" she commanded.

"Is she the star of the show or something?" Mortimer snickered.

"No, but she thinks she is," Greta frowned. "And she's only in the fifth grade. Just wait till she's in eighth grade. She won't want anyone else playing in the whole recital except her."

Second-grader Terry Terracotta took out his clarinet and asked if someone would play a B flat for him so he could tune his clarinet.

"How can I hear to tune my violin if you're playing, too?" Gloria snapped at him.

"Well, I'm going on before you," explained Terry. "So I should tune up before you, right?"

"No!" Gloria said. She looked down her nose at Terry. "I'm going to be a famous concert violinist someday," she told him.

Greta became angry when she saw Terry's eyes fill with tears. "You won't have any fans if you're so mean," she told Gloria. Terry brightened up, and Greta smiled.

Gloria glared at Greta. Then in a huff, she turned and walked to the window. "What's that?" Gloria asked, pointing to a tiny gold violin sitting in Samantha's violin case.

"It's my lucky violin charm," Samantha answered. "It's going to help me get through my solo without one mistake."

"You'll need it," snickered Gloria. "Especially since you don't have any talent." Samantha's face fell.

"Don't listen to her, Samantha," said Mortimer. "You're really good."

"Thanks," said Samantha. She tried hard to smile.

Just then Miss Harmony entered the room. "Well, music makers, are we ready to perform?" she said. "Let's go over the list of the order you'll be playing in."

Miss Harmony turned to a group of her youngest students. "Let's see, Margaret, you're first with 'Twinkle, Twinkle,'" she said. Margaret, a first-grader, stepped forward to have her violin tuned.

When Miss Harmony got to Gloria she said, "Oh, don't we look grown-up in our high heels." Gloria proudly looked down at her shoes, which had very thin heels. Greta rolled her eyes.

Miss Harmony tuned Gloria's violin then called out Samantha's name.

"But Samantha's playing before me, isn't she?" cried Gloria.

"No, Samantha took on an extremely difficult piece for the concert," said Miss Harmony. "And since she's done so well, we're putting her on at the end of the first half of the recital." She beamed at Samantha. "I'll tune the older students' instruments during the intermission."

Gloria was furious. "But, but . . . Samantha's in the fourth grade," she stammered. "I'm older. I should go after her." Some of the other fifth-grade students weren't happy about Samantha going on last, either. When they heard Gloria complaining, they began grumbling, too.

"Yeah," said Paul Pearly, another fifth-grader. "That doesn't seem fair."

"I think I'm better than Samantha anyway," boasted Fred Flat. "Why should she play ahead of me?"

Miss Harmony stood up and clapped her hands. "Now, now, NOW!" she said firmly. "'Better' isn't a word we like to use in this school. The program is set. And that's that."

The grumbling stopped, but several of the fifth-graders still frowned at Samantha. Finally everyone finished tuning their instruments, and the recital was about to start. It was then that Samantha discovered that her lucky violin charm was missing.

"Oh, no! My lucky charm is gone," she cried. "I can't play without it."

"Yes, yes, yes. Of course you can," Miss Harmony said. "Don't be silly, dear. Luck doesn't make you a good player. Practice does. You're ready to play this piece, believe me."

"I just hope I can get through my solo okay," Samantha fretted.

Miss Harmony was right. Samantha played her piece perfectly. Miss Harmony clapped loudly as Samantha took a bow.

"You were swell!" Mortimer told Samantha during intermission.

"No one would have known you had a handicap," laughed Peter.

"Thanks, guys." Samantha blushed. "Wow. I didn't make one mistake. I guess I learned something today. I don't need that lucky charm after all."

When the recital was over, the students all gathered in the warm-up room. "Follow me, students," Miss Harmony called out. "The janitor is going to clean the warm-up room while we have our pictures taken in the recital hall."

First the photographer took a group photo; then he took photos by grade, starting with eighth-graders first. When the photographer had finished, the students headed back to the warm-up room. Everyone began putting away their instruments and collecting their things to go home. "Look, Samantha," said Greta, pointing to Samantha's violin case across the room. "Your lucky charm."

Sure enough, the missing violin charm was sitting on top of Samantha's violin case.

"Whoever took your charm must have brought it back while you were having your pictures taken," said Mortimer.

Samantha started to walk toward her case. "Samantha, stop!" cried Peter. "Wait here a minute. I think I know who took your charm."

"You do?" asked Samantha. "Who?"

"Gloria," Peter answered, turning to Gloria.

How does Peter know Gloria took Samantha's lucky charm?

Solution
The Case of the
Missing Charm

"That's ridiculous," Gloria declared. "Why do you think it was me?"

"Because you look so grown-up," said Peter, snickering.

"That doesn't make a lot of sense, Peter," said Miss Harmony. "Now be serious."

"Remember, Miss Harmony? You said Gloria looked so grown-up in her new heels," said Peter.

"I get it," said Mortimer, pointing to the footprints in the deep carpet.

"Yes!" said Greta. "I see! Look. The shoe prints have a tiny heel."

Everyone looked at the footprints going to and from Samantha's violin case. The janitor had vacuumed after the recital. The tiny heel footprints were the only foot-prints on that part of the carpet.

"Why don't you walk beside them, Gloria, and we'll see if they match," said Miss Harmony.

The shoe prints were exactly the same. Gloria was caught by her new grown-up shoes.

"It wasn't fair that she got to end the first half," Gloria whined. "I thought she would mess up without her lucky charm."

"Oh, shame, Gloria!" said Miss Harmony. "That was very childish."

"Yeah, Gloria may have looked grown-up in her heels," said Greta, "but she acted like a baby when she took Samantha's lucky charm."

Your favorite game is a mystery series!

created by
Parker C. Hinter

The more things change...the more confused Amber Brown gets!

FOREVER AMBER BROWN

by Paula Danziger

Amber Brown has already gone through a lot of changes — but now Max, her mother's boyfriend, is asking her mom to marry him! Why can't things just stay the same *forever*?

Coming in August to bookstores everywhere.

Have you read Amber's other adventures?
AMBER BROWN IS NOT A CRAYON
YOU CAN'T EAT YOUR CHICKEN POX, AMBER BROWN
AMBER BROWN GOES FOURTH
AMBER BROWN WANTS EXTRA CREDIT

Creepy, weird, wacky and funny things happen to the Bailey School Kids!™ Collect and read them all!

The Adventures of
THE BAILEY SCHOOL KIDS®